The Ups and Downs of Mouse and Mole

Joyce Dunbar

Illustrated by Alison de Vere

CORGI PUPS

THE UPS AND DOWNS OF MOUSE AND MOLE
A CORGI PUPS BOOK

First publicaton in Great Britain

PRINTING HISTORY
Corgi Pups edition published 2001

ISBN 0 552 54944 4

Set in 18/25 Bembo MT Schoolbook by
Phoenix Typesetting, Ilkley, West Yorkshire

Corgi Pups Books are published by Transworld Publishers,
61–63 Uxbridge Road, Ealing, London W5 5SA,
a division of the Random House Group Ltd,
in Australia by Random House Australia (Pty) Ltd,
20 Alfred Street, Milsons Point, Sydney, NSW 2061, Australia
in New Zealand by Random House New Zealand Ltd,
18 Poland Road, Glenfield, Auckland 10, New Zealand
and in South Africa by Random House (Pty) Ltd,
Endulini, 5a Jubilee Road, Parktown 2193, South Africa

Printed and bound in Denmark by
Nørhaven Paperback, Viborg

Contents

Series Reading Consultant: Prue Goodwin,
Reading and Language Information Centre,
University of Reading

The Secret of Happiness

The light peeped in through the curtains. Day was beginning to dawn. Suddenly, Mole woke up.

"Mouse! Mouse! Wake up!" he cried.

"I have," said Mouse, nearly jumping out of his skin. "I am."

"I had a dream," said Mole.

"So did I," said Mouse. "Now can I go back and finish it?"

"But, Mouse! You don't understand. I dreamt that I knew the secret of happiness!"

"The secret of happiness is a good night's sleep," grumbled Mouse.

"No, Mouse. You must listen. I really did dream that I had found the secret of happiness. And it was so obvious, as if I'd always known it."

"Tell me after breakfast,"
said Mouse.

"*I can't*," wailed Mole. "*I've
forgotten it!*"

"Go back to sleep," said
Mouse. "Then you might dream
it again."

"And I might not," said Mole.
"I might forget that I ever
dreamt it at all."

"Well, we may as well have breakfast," said Mouse, giving up and putting on his dressing gown.

Mole put on his dressing gown too, scratching his head all the while, trying to remember his dream.

"Was it a pair of warm slippers?" asked Mouse, putting on his own warm slippers.

"No, it wasn't," said Mole.

"Perhaps it was a nice cup of tea," said Mouse, putting on the kettle.

"No, it wasn't," said Mole.

"Perhaps it was early-
morning birdsong," said Mouse,
opening a window wide.

"No, it wasn't," said Mole. "It was none of these things. It sort of bubbled up, it sort of billowed, it sort of bloomed, from somewhere deep inside me. And it was so easy, Mouse, so easy in the dream."

All day long Mole prowled around, scratching his head, trying to remember what it was. He was still scratching when Rat turned up for tea, with Hedgehog and Rabbit close behind.

"What's up, Mole?" asked
Rat.

"I found the best thing in the
world and I lost it," burbled
Mole. "I shan't be happy again
till I find it."

"Mole's always losing things,"
said Hedgehog.

"What is it this time?" asked
Rabbit.

Mouse tried to explain.

Rat had an idea. "I know
how to help him to find it," he
said. "We must all try to jog his

memory. Now, Mole, what in the
world would make you happy?"

"Well . . ." said Mole, looking
thoughtfully at Rat's hat.

"How about this four-leaf
clover I found?" said Hedgehog.
"It's sure to bring you lots of
luck."

"Why, thank you, Hedgehog," said Mole.

"And I've brought a summer pudding to share," said Rabbit. "You can have the biggest helping."

"Why, thank you, Rabbit," said Mole.

"And I promise you a ride on my bicycle!" said Rat.

"Oh, I couldn't," protested Mole. "But I have always liked your green hat."

"All right then, Mole. Here you are. My one and only green hat. Love it dearly."

"Anything else?" asked
Mouse.

"I wouldn't mind a stool for
my feet and a cushion for my
back," said Mole.

"Whatever you want, Mole,"
they all fussed. "Your wish is
our command."

Before long, there sat Mole, his feet on a stool, his back on a cushion, his stomach full of summer pudding. "Mmmmm," he sighed, patting his hat, twirling his four-leaf clover.

"Mmmmm . . ."

Then, suddenly, it came: it sort of billowed, it sort of blossomed, it sort of bubbled up from somewhere deep inside him. A feeling of complete happiness. A smile spread over his face. "I've got it!" he said. "I've got it!"

"Well?" said his friends.

"The secret of happiness
is . . ." Mole began.
"Yes?" said his friends.

". . . is . . . izz . . . izzzzzzzzzzz,"
went Mole.

But before he could say what it was, he fell into a deep, happy sleep.

A Rainy Day

The rain was crying down the
window. "It's raining, Mouse,"
said Mole.

"I know."

"It rained all yesterday too."

"I know."

"And the day before that as well."

"I know."

"It's been raining for as long
as I can remember."

"And me."

"I wish it would stop."

"So do I."

"I'm going to tell it to stop."

"You can try."

"STOP RAINING!" shouted Mole.

The rain rained on.

"STOP RAINING!" shouted Mole again, stamping his foot at the same time.

But the rain rained on.

"I think it's raining on purpose to annoy me," said Mole.

"Oh, I shouldn't think so, Mole," said Mouse.

"Let's go outside to show the rain what's what," said Mole.

"That's a good idea," said Mouse. "Let's show it who's who."

So Mouse and Mole put on
their mackintoshes and galoshes
and sou'westers. Then they stood
outside in the rain.

"It's chucking it down!" said Mouse.

"Bucketing down!" said Mole.

"STOP RAINING!" they shouted together.

But the rain rained on.

"I once heard of a rain dance," said Mouse. "We could do a stop-raining dance."

So Mouse and Mole did a stop-raining dance. Mouse rattled a stick on the fence and Mole banged on a dustbin lid.

But the rain rained on.

"Let's try a stop-raining song to go with the stop-raining dance," said Mouse.

"Rain rain go away,
Come again another day,"

they sang to the rain.

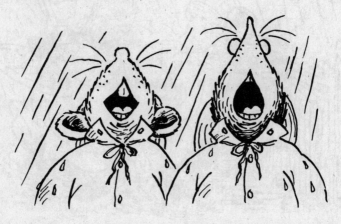

But the rain rained on.

"Let's try something different.
Let's be nice to the rain," said
Mouse.

"How do we do that?" asked
Mole.

"Oh, rain! Oh, lovely rain. We love you, rain. But now we've had enough. Stop, rain. You need a rest," said Mouse.

"I get the idea," said Mole, opening his arms wide. "Let's hug the rain."

They both hugged the rain.

"Let's blow kisses to the rain,"
said Mouse.

They both blew kisses to the
rain. The rain kissed them both
back. It rained big wet
raindrops on their faces.

Mouse blinked happily.
So did Mole.
"We could always make
friends with the rain," said
Mouse. "We could have some
fun and make a moat."

So Mouse and Mole started to
dig a moat. "Why didn't we
think of this before?" they said.

They worked for hours and hours. They forgot about everything else.

Rat came walking by. "What are you doing?" he asked.

"We're making a moat," said
Mouse.

"It looks like a trench to me,"
said Rat.

"But it won't be a trench
when it's finished. It will be a
moat. With all this rain raining
down, it will soon fill up with
water. Then we can make a
drawbridge."

"What rain?" asked Rat.

Mouse looked up. Mole
looked up. They held out their
paws. They felt not a single drop
of rain.

"The rain stopped ages ago,"
said Rat. "That's why I'm out
for a walk."

"There's nothing else for it,"
said Mouse. "We shall have to
do a rain dance. Come on, Rat,
join in."

"Pour, pour, rain, rain,
Chuck it, bucket,
down again,"

they chanted together.
Out came the smiling sun.

A Sad Moment

Mouse lit an applewood fire. He made a pot of pea soup.

Mole sat by the fire and warmed his paws. He sniffed the soup and smacked his chops.

"Here you are," said Mouse, passing him a bowlful.

"My favourite soup," said Mole.

"And here's a spoon to eat it with," said Mouse.

"My favourite spoon, too," said Mole.

Suddenly, Mole put down his
bowl of soup, dashed over to
the door and stood outside in
the cold.

"Why are you standing outside?" asked Mouse. "You are letting in all the cold air."

Mole shivered. His teeth chattered. He stood there feeling cold and hungry.

"What was that for?" asked Mouse.

"Because there is nothing so good as a warm fire when you are cold. And there is nothing so tasty as pea soup when you are hungry," said Mole. "Now I can enjoy it all the more."

Mole warmed himself up. He started to eat his soup. He gave a big, happy sigh. "This is the happiest moment of my life," he said.

"Good," said Mouse.

Then Mole gave a loud sob.

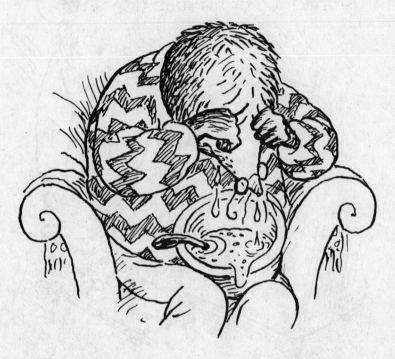

"What's the matter?" asked
Mouse.

"This is a very sad moment,"
said Mole.

"But you just said it was the happiest moment of your life," said Mouse.

"That's just it," said Mole. "It means I have never been so happy before. It means I will never be so happy again. What could be sadder than that?"

"You never know what tomorrow might bring," said Mouse.

"I will be one day older," said Mole.

"But you will be younger
than you will be on the day
after tomorrow," said Mouse.
"You are never so old as you are
going to be."

"That's a thought," said Mole.

56

"So at this moment I'm the youngest I'll ever be."

"That's right," said Mouse.

"Moments are funny things," said Mole. "They never keep still."

"They don't," said Mouse.
"They are over before you know
where you are."

"I wish I could keep them in
my pocket and take them out
every so often," said Mole.

"I know what you mean,"
said Mouse.

"What do I mean?" asked
Mole, starting on his soup again.

"Well, when it is wild and wintry outside, like now, don't you long for a moment in summer, lazing away in a hammock?" said Mouse.

"I do," slurped Mole.

"And then, when it's summer, don't you yearn for a moment in spring, with the sight of the very first daffodil?" said Mouse.

"Yes, I do," slurped Mole.

"And then, in the spring, don't you pine for a moment in autumn, chasing the falling leaves?" said Mouse.

"That I do," slurped Mole.

"And in the autumn, don't you wish for a wild and wintry moment, like now?" sighed Mouse.

"Oh, I do," agreed Mole, licking his snout. "There is nothing like the nowness of now."

"And in the nowness of now, what could be better than to sit by the fire with a bowl full of pea soup," went on Mouse.

"Mine isn't full," said Mole. "Mine's half empty."

"That all depends on the way you look at it," said Mouse. "I would say it was half full."

"I like it full-to-the top full," said Mole.

"Here, have some more," said Mouse, filling up his bowl.

"Mouse, I was wrong about the happiest moment of my life. This one is even happier. Pass me the salt please, Mouse."

And Mouse did.

THE END